j I CAN READ Avengers
Macri, Thomas,
These are the Avengers /
9781614792536

World of Reading

THESE ARE THE AVENGERS

Adapted by **Thomas Macri**

Illustrated by **Mike Norton** *and* **Hi-Fi Design**

Based on the Marvel comic book series **The Mighty Avengers**

ABDO
Spotlight

New York

WWW.ABDOPUBLISHING.COM

Reinforced library bound edition published in 2015 by Spotlight, a division of ABDO PO Box 398166, Minneapolis, Minnesota 55439. Spotlight produces high-quality reinforced library bound editions for schools and libraries. Published by Marvel Press, an imprint of Disney Book Group.

Printed in the United States of America, North Mankato, Minnesota.
052014
072014

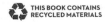

marvelkids.com

THIS BOOK CONTAINS RECYCLED MATERIALS

LIBRARY OF CONGRESS CATALOGING-IN-PUBLICATION DATA

This title was previously cataloged with the following information:

Macri, Thomas.
These are the Avengers / adapted by Thomas Macri ; illustrated by Mike Norton and Hi-Fi Design.
p. cm. -- (World of reading. Level 1)
Summary: Describes the powers and abilities of the members of the Avengers, including Ant-Man, Hulk, and Thor.
1. Avengers (Fictitious characters)--Juvenile fiction. 2. Superheroes--Juvenile fiction. I. Norton, Mike, ill. II. Hi-Fi Colour Design, ill. III. Title. IV. Series.
PZ7.M24731Te 2012
[Fic]--dc23

2012288905

978-1-61479-253-6 (Reinforced Library Bound Edition)

ABDO
Spotlight
A Division of ABDO
www.abdopublishing.com

These are the Avengers.

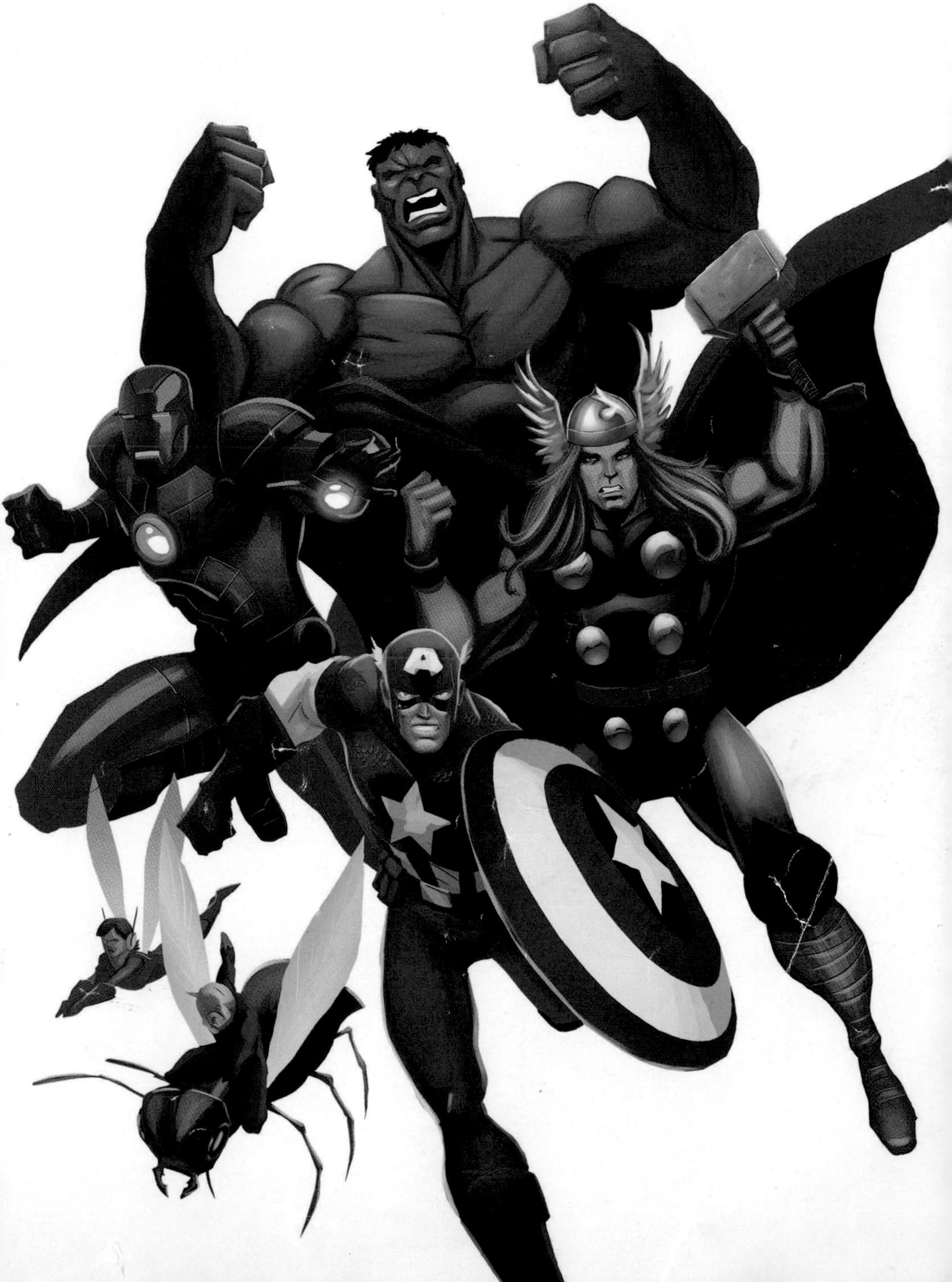

The Avengers are a team of Super Heroes.

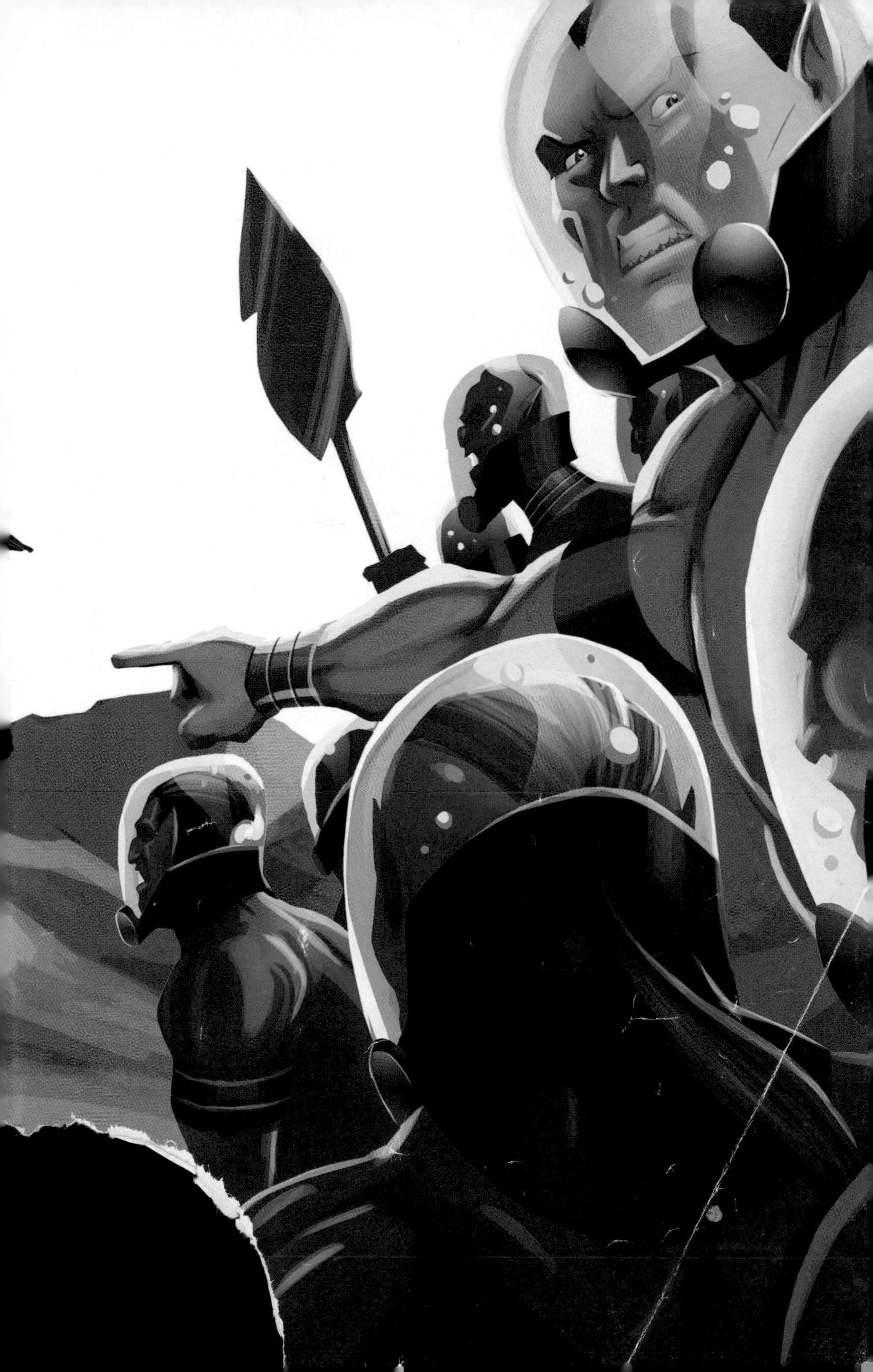

Six Super Heroes are Avengers.

Each has a power.

Captain America is strong.

He has a shield.
His shield
cannot break.

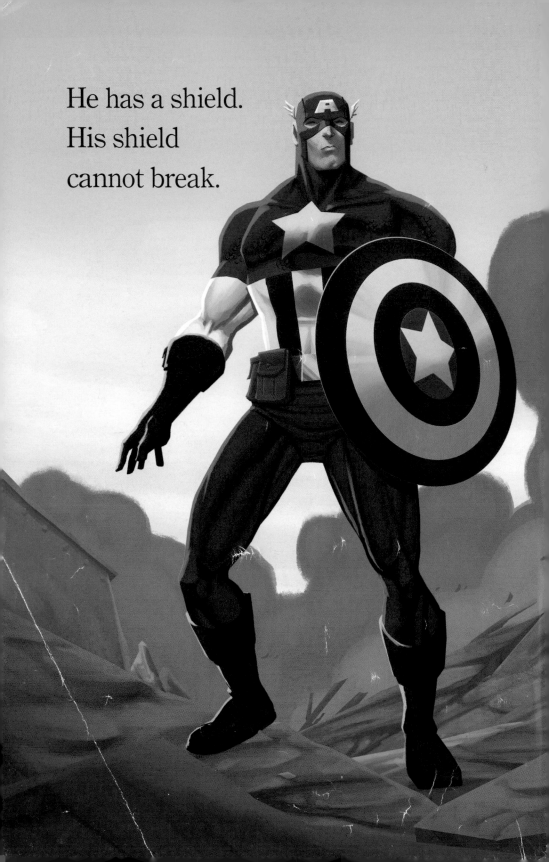

He throws his shield
to stop bad guys.

It flies back.

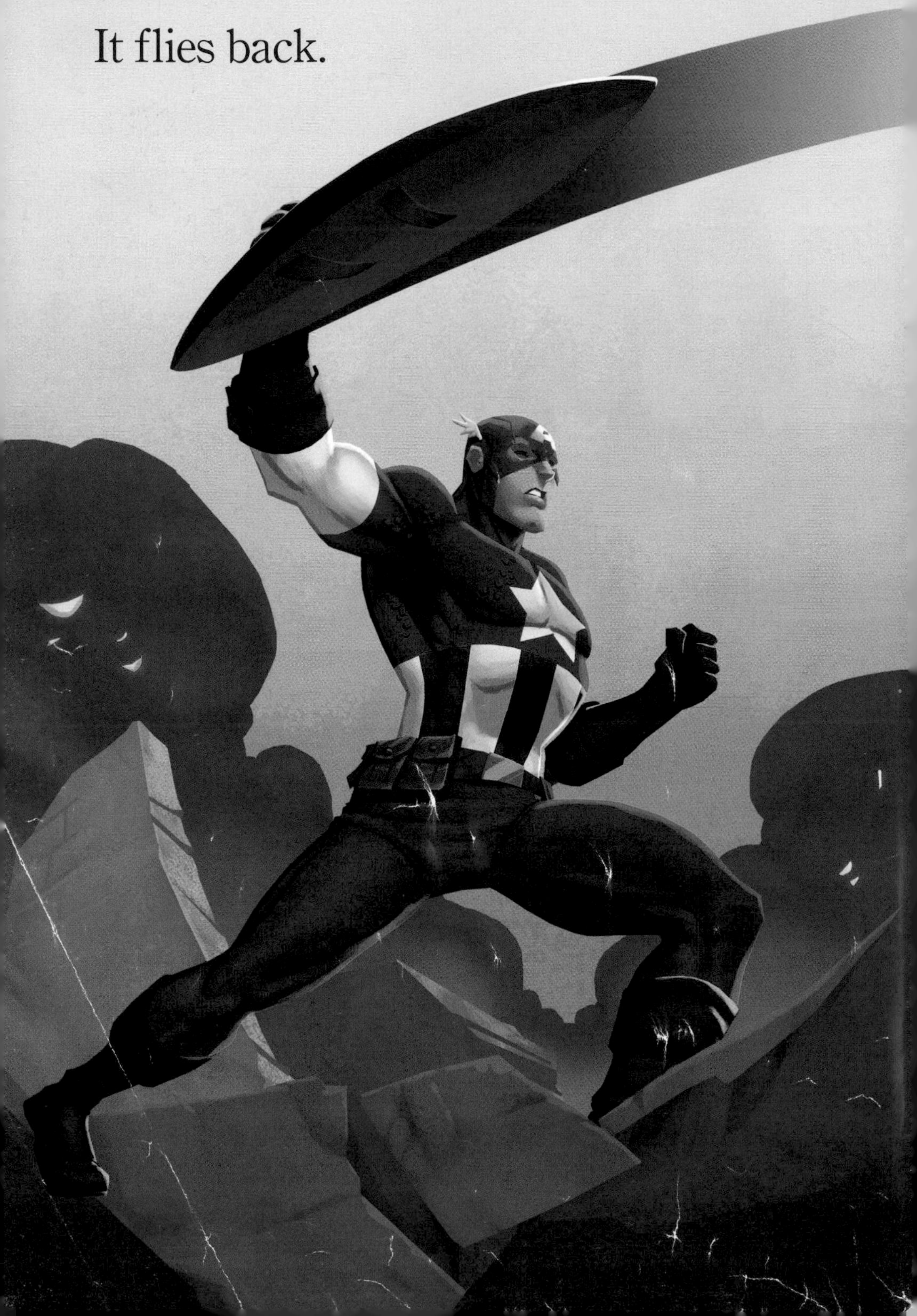

Ant-Man is an Avenger, too.
He can become
as small as an ant.

Ant-Man can speak to bugs.
They help him win
his fights.

Ant-Man can also
make himself big.

Ant-Man calls himself
Giant-Man when he is big.

Ant-Man has a partner.
She is called Wasp.

Wasp is like Ant-Man.
She can become small.

She has wings.
She can fly.
She can sting.

This is the Hulk.

He is an Avenger, too.

The Hulk is big.
He is green.
He is very strong..

He can even smash bricks.

This is Thor.
Thor is also
an Avenger.

Thor has a hammer.
He uses it to fly.

Thor slams his hammer
to make thunder.

Thor throws his hammer.
It always comes back to him.

Iron Man is
an Avenger.

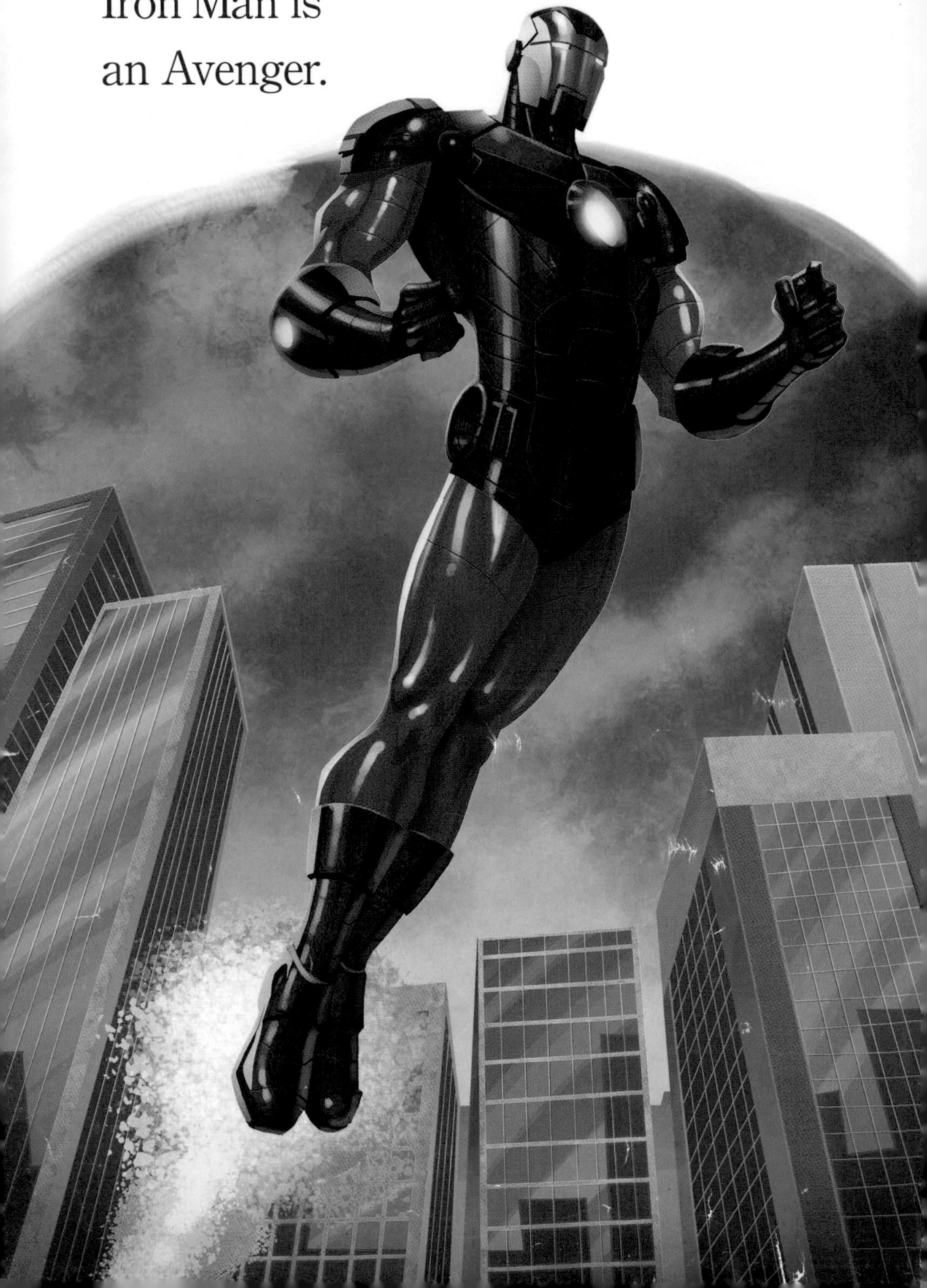

Iron Man is not a robot.
He is a man
in an iron suit.
His name is Tony.

Tony made the suit.

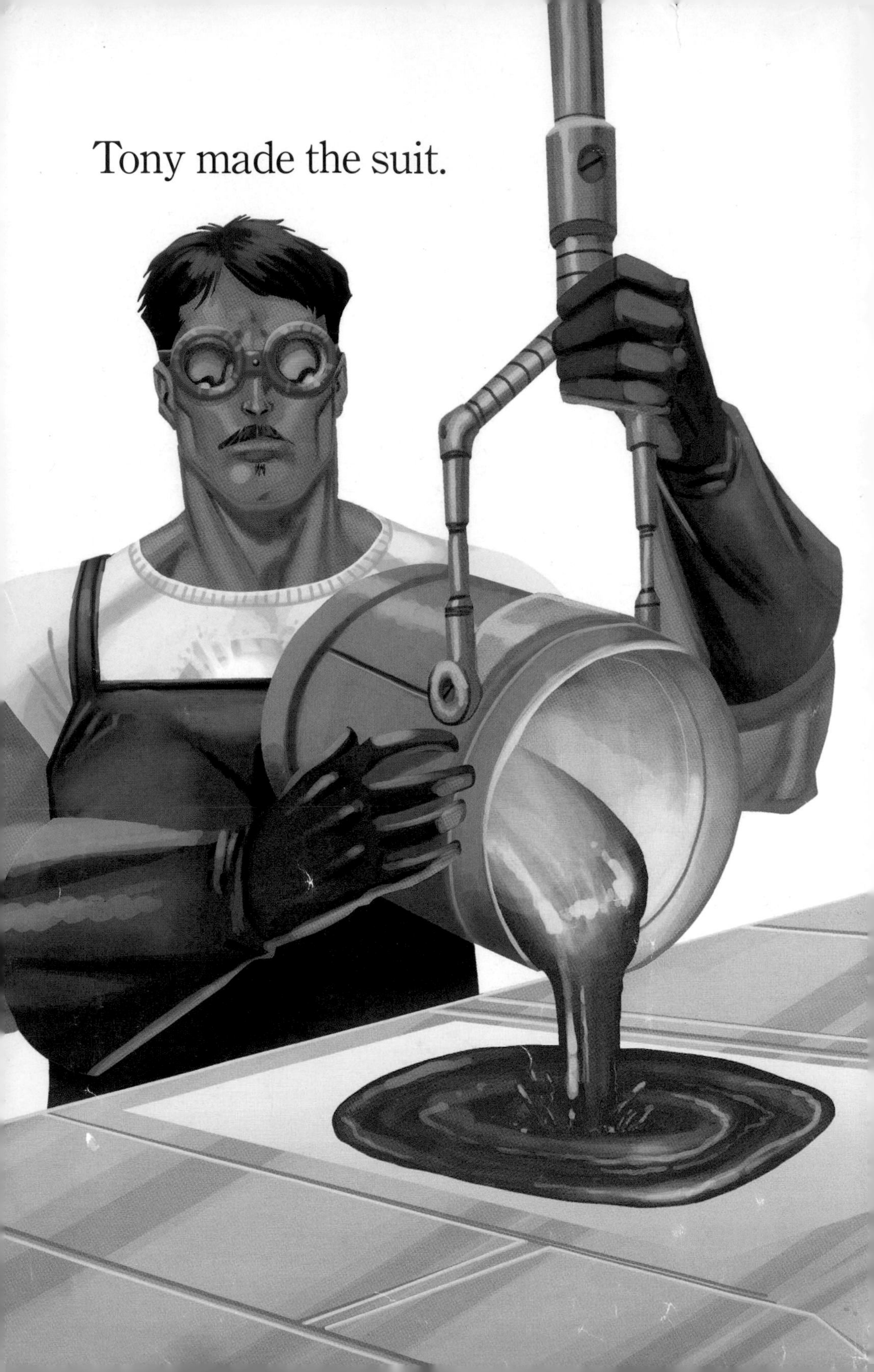

Tony is safer in the suit.
The suit is full of power.

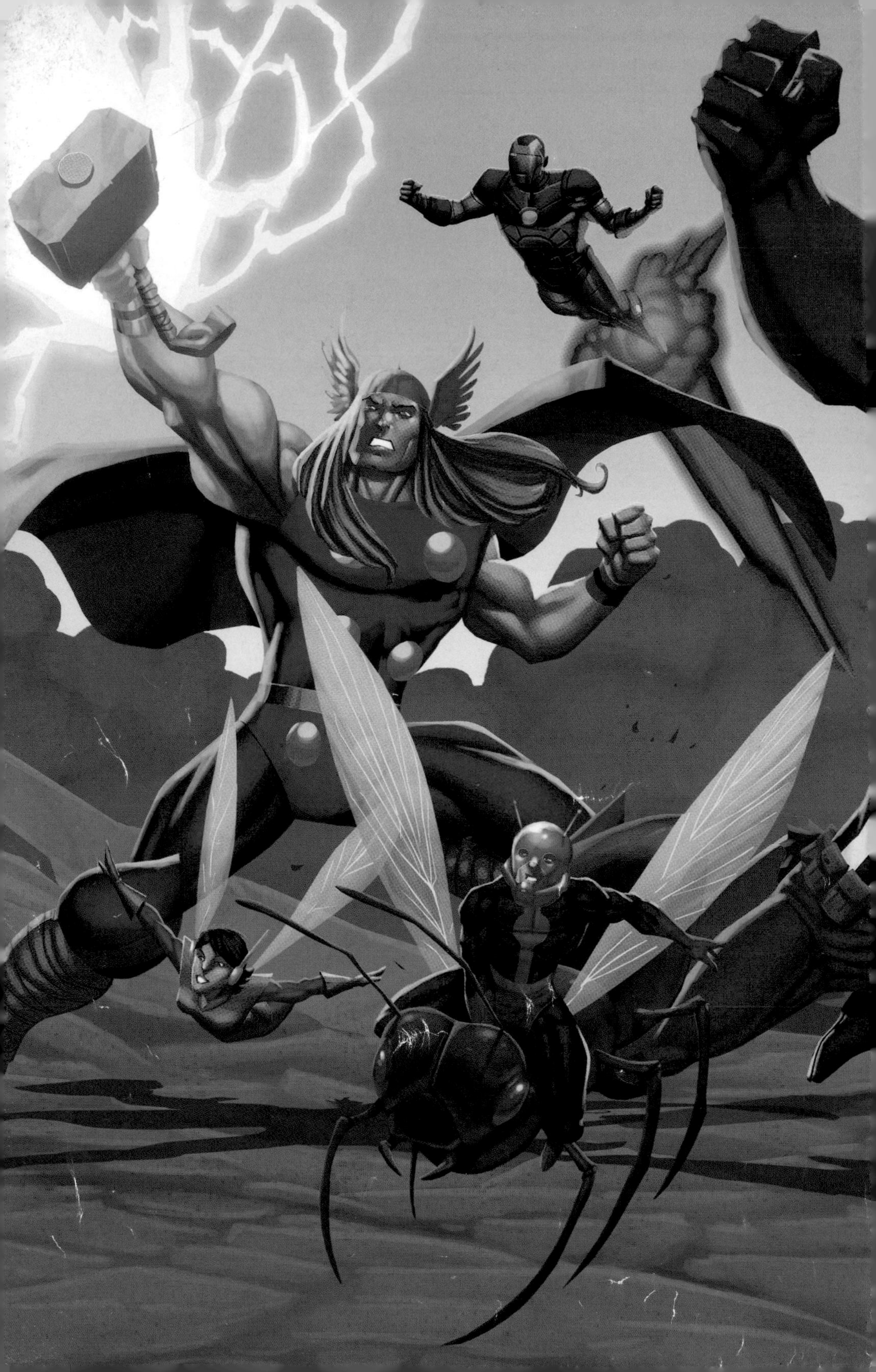

Each hero is strong.

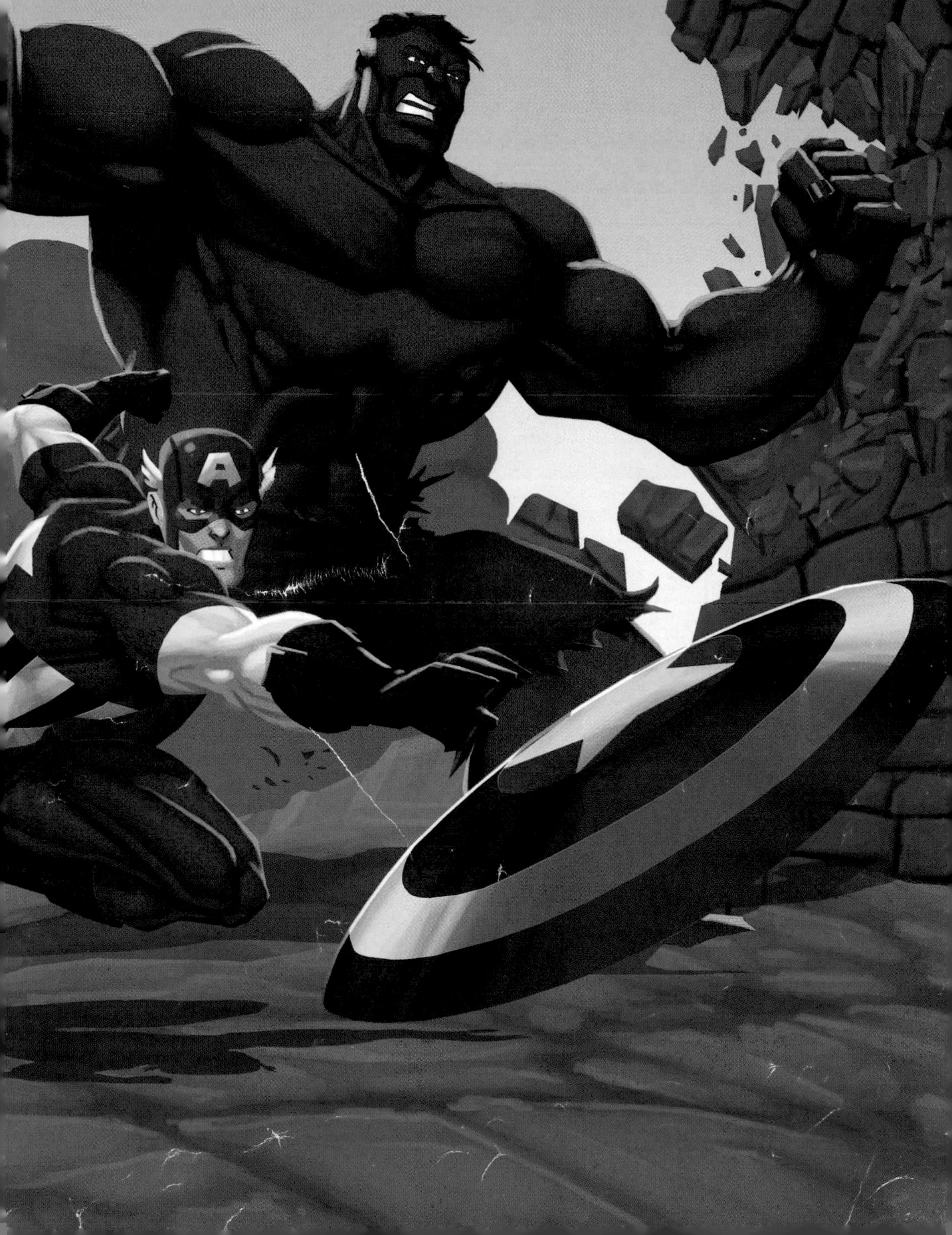

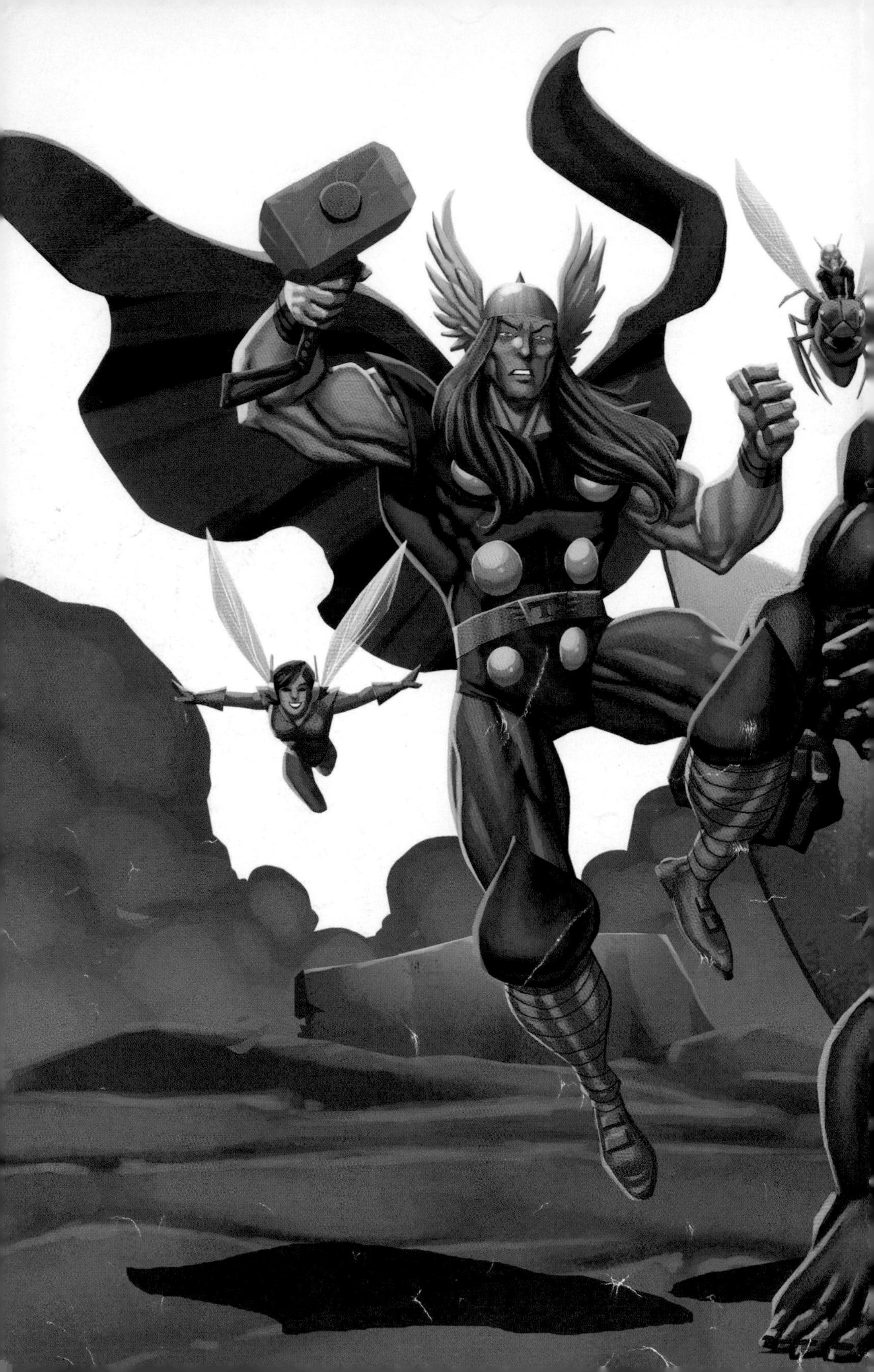

As a team they are stronger.

These are the Avengers.

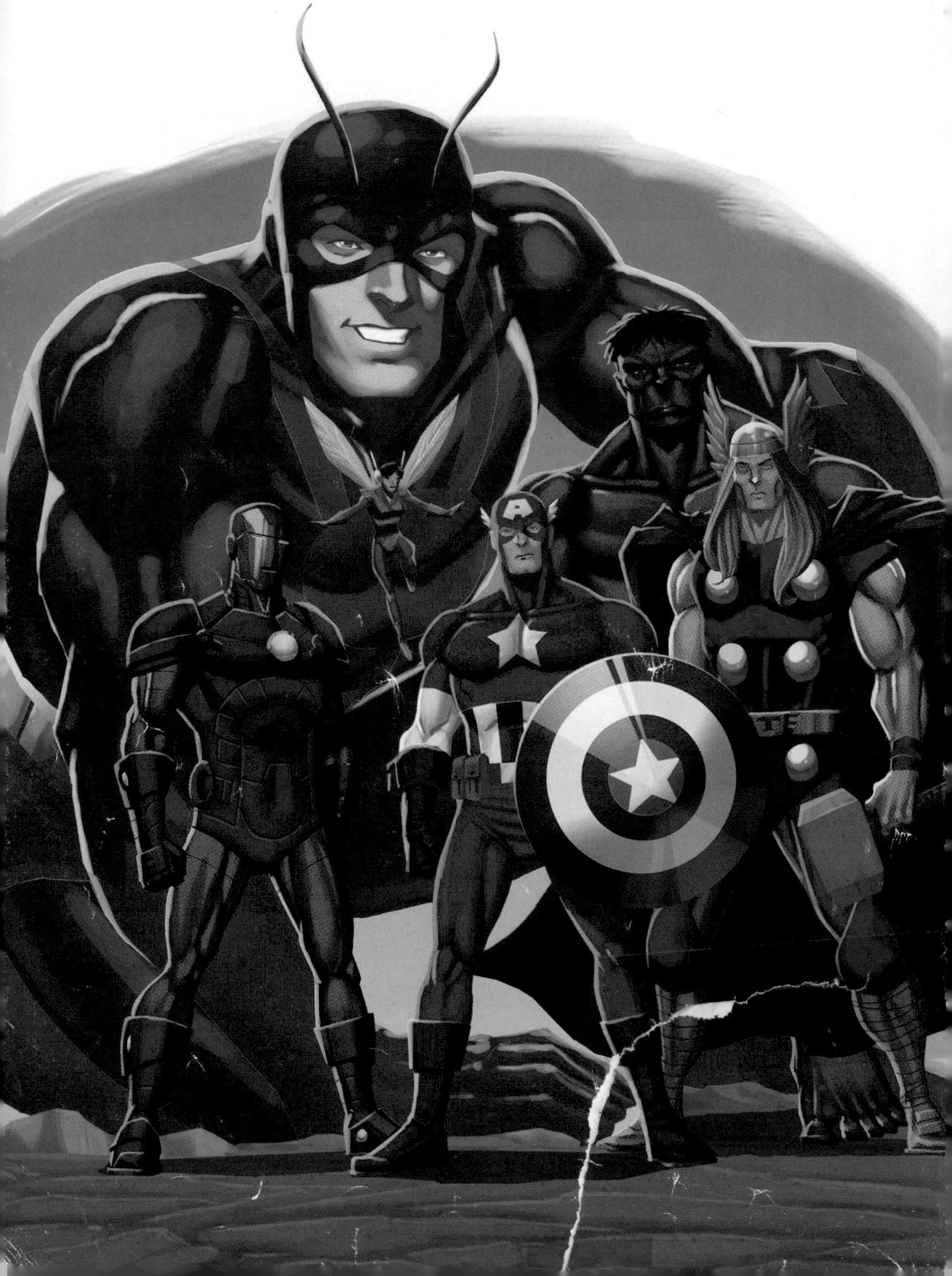